RIPLEY'S

RBI

FACT OR FICTION?

BUREAU OF INVESTIGATION

PUBLISHING

Copyright © 2010 by Ripley Entertainment, Inc.

All rights reserved.
Ripley's, Believe It or Not!, and Ripley's Believe It or Not!
are registered trademarks of Ripley Entertainment Inc.

ISBN : 978-1-893951-56-3

10 9 8 7 6 5 4 3 2 1

Design: Dynamo Limited
Text: Kay Wilkins
Interior Artwork: Ailin Chambers

For information regarding permission,
write to VP Intellectual Property, Ripley Entertainment Inc.,
Suite 188, 7576 Kingspointe Parkway, Orlando, Florida 32819

Email: publishing@ripleys.com
www.ripleysrbi.com

Manufactured in Dallas, PA, United States
in August/2010 by Offset Paperback Manufacturers

1st printing

All characters appearing in this work (pages 1-118) are fictitious and
any resemblance to real persons, living or dead, is purely coincidental.

WARNING: Some of the activities undertaken by the RBI and others in this book
should not be attempted by anyone without the necessary training and supervision.

_____

Collector card picture credits: t/r Sipa Press/Rex Features;
b/l Anja Niedringhaus/AP/Press Association Images

WINGS
OF FEAR

PUBLISHING

a Jim Pattison Company

INTRODUCING THE RBI

Hidden away on a small island off the East Coast of the United States is Ripley High —a unique school for children who possess extraordinary talents.

Located in the former home of Robert Ripley—creator of the world-famous Ripley's Believe It or Not!—the school takes students who all share a secret. Although they look like you or me, they have amazing skills: the ability to conduct electricity, superhuman strength, or control over the weather—these are just a few of the talents the Ripley High School students possess.

The very best of these talented kids have been invited to join a top secret agency—Ripley's Bureau of Investigation: the RBI. This elite group operates from a hi-tech underground base hidden deep beneath the school. From here, the talented teen agents are sent on dangerous missions around the world, investigating sightings of fantastical creatures and strange occurrences. Join them on their incredible adventures as they seek out the weird and the wonderful, and try to separate fact from fiction ...

RIPLEY

The spirit of Robert Ripley lives on in **RIPLEY**, a supercomputer that stores the database—all Ripley's bizarre collections, and information on all the artifacts and amazing discoveries made by the RBI. Featuring a fully interactive holographic Ripley as its interface, RIPLEY gives the agents info on their missions and sends them invaluable data on their R-phones.

THE TEACHERS

▶▶ Mr. Cain

The agents' favorite teacher, Mr. Cain, runs the RBI—under the guise of a Museum Club—and coordinates all the agents' missions.

▶▶ Dr. Maxwell

The only other teacher at the school who knows about the RBI. Dr. Maxwell equips the agents for their missions with cutting-edge gadgets from his lab.

MEET THE RBI TEAM

As well as having amazing talents, each of the seven members of the RBI has expert knowledge in their own individual fields of interest. All with different skills, the team supports each other at school and while out on missions, where the three most suitable agents are chosen for each case.

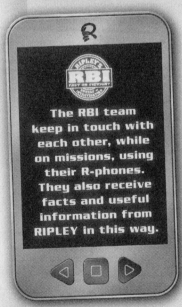

The RBI team keep in touch with each other, while on missions, using their R-phones. They also receive facts and useful information from RIPLEY in this way.

▶▶ KOBE

NAME : Kobe Shakur

AGE : 15

SKILLS : Excellent tracking and endurance skills, tribal knowledge, and telepathic abilities

NOTES : Kobe's parents grew up in different African tribes. Kobe has amazing tracking capabilities and is an expert on native cultures across the world. He can also tell the entire history of a person or object just by touching it.

▶▶ ZIA

NAME : Zia Mendoza

AGE : 13

SKILLS : Possesses magnetic and electrical powers. Can predict the weather

NOTES : The only survivor of a tropical storm that destroyed her village when she was a baby. Zia doesn't yet fully understand her abilities but she can predict, and sometimes control, the weather. Her presence can also affect electrical equipment.

▶▶ MAX

NAME : Max Johnson

AGE : 14

SKILLS : Computer genius and inventor

NOTES : Max, from Las Vegas, loves computer games and anything electrical. He spends most of his spare time inventing robots. Max hates school but he loves spending time helping Dr. Maxwell come up with new gadgets.

▶▶ KATE

▶▶ ALEK

NAME : Kate Jones

AGE : 14

SKILLS : Computer-like memory, extremely clever, and ability to master languages in minutes

NOTES : Raised at Oxford University in England by her history professor and part-time archaeologist uncle, Kate memorized every book in the University library after reading them only once!

NAME : Alek Filipov

AGE : 15

SKILL : Contortionist with amazing physical strength

NOTES : Alek is a member of the Russian under-16 Olympic gymnastics team and loves sports and competitions. He is much bigger than the other agents, and although he seems quiet and serious much of the time, he has a wicked sense of humor.

▶▶ LI

NAME : Li Yong

AGE : 15

SKILL : Musical genius with pitch-perfect hearing and the ability to mimic any sound

NOTES : Li grew up in a wealthy family in Beijing, China, and joined Ripley High later than the other RBI agents. She has a highly developed sense of hearing and can imitate any sound she hears.

▶▶ JACK

NAME : Jack Stevens

AGE : 14

SKILLS : Can "talk" to animals and has expert survival skills

NOTES : Jack grew up on an animal park in the Australian outback. He has always shared a strong bond with animals and can communicate with any creature— and loves to eat weird food!

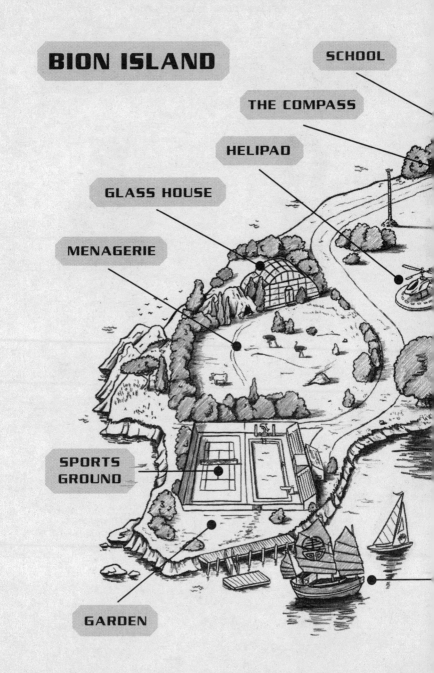

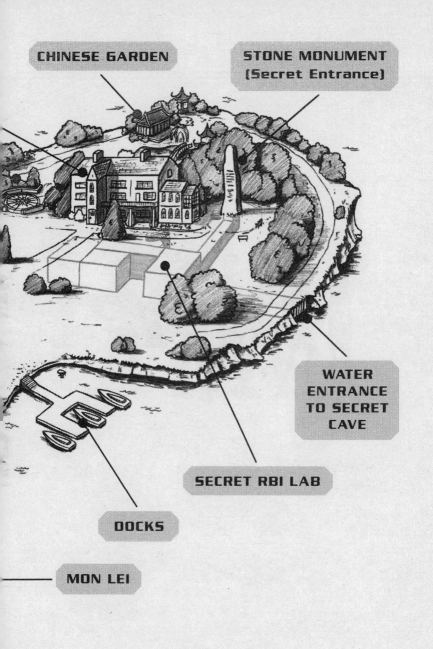

CHINESE GARDEN

STONE MONUMENT
(Secret Entrance)

WATER
ENTRANCE
TO SECRET
CAVE

SECRET RBI LAB

DOCKS

MON LEI

Prologue

It was almost 9:30 and Abby was going to be late for work—again! She rushed out of the subway station, taking the steps up to street level two at a time. Abby had tried so hard to be on time, but last night she had had dinner with her best friend Clare, who she hadn't seen for ages, and they had talked for hours. Then, when her alarm went off this morning, she had just been *so* tired!

As she rushed along the sidewalk, Abby tried to work out how she was going to get everything done before the Ripley's museum—where she worked—opened in half an hour.

Suddenly, Abby heard a strange noise. She pulled her cell phone from her pocket to see if someone was calling. It wasn't the noise her phone normally made, but it would be just like Clare to have changed the ringtone while she wasn't looking. But the noise wasn't her phone. It grew louder and louder—a high-pitched whine, like an airplane makes just before its engines kick in. Abby looked up to see if there was a plane in trouble, shielding her eyes from the morning sun. As she did so, a large shadow appeared. Huge wings blocked out the sun, and warmth like a fire swallowed up the cool morning breeze. Bright flames lit up the sky as a large flying creature shot past above Abby's head.

Thinking quickly, she switched her phone

to camera mode and tried to get some film of the strange thing. Nobody would believe her about this unless they saw it! Running down the street she filmed until the *thing*, whatever it was, disappeared from view.

Replaying the video Abby looked closely at the screen. It almost seemed as if the creature was surrounded by fire. Abby felt herself go cold with fear. What could it possibly have been?

Closing her phone, Abby ran the rest of the way to work—terrified that the creature might return.

1

Kismet

"I just find it so peaceful here," said Jack. He and Zia were in the Ripley High menagerie. This was home to all the unbelievable animals that Robert Ripley had found on his travels, along with all those that the RBI had discovered on their missions.

Zia listened to the orchestra of animal noises—bird songs, monkey calls, and barking dogs—and wondered how Jack could think that it was peaceful.

"It's a little bit cold this morning," said Zia, as she pulled her jacket tighter around her.

"It reminds me of home," said Jack, and then Zia understood. He had grown up on an animal park in Australia, so all sorts of weird and wonderful animal noises would have surrounded him there. "Apart from the cold that is!" he added.

Jack was feeding the monkey-pig—a pig with the face of a monkey—and Zia was amazed at how gentle and caring he was with the animals. Just then, there was a blur of fur as something whizzed past them.

▶▶ A piglet born in China in 2008 had the face of a monkey. The newborn had two thin lips, a small nose, two big eyes, and its rear legs were considerably longer than its front ones. The shocked owner said that his son liked to play with the creature.

"Oh no, that was Kismet," Zia shrieked.

Kismet, the winged cat, was Zia's favorite animal in the menagerie. Whenever she came with Jack to see the animals, she always made sure that she spent some time with the little creature. She ran off after her and found Buster, the two-nosed dog, sitting at the bottom of one of the trees, looking up expectantly and barking.

"Bad Buster," scolded Zia, as she looked up into the branches to see the multicolored face of Kismet peering down at her. Carefully, she climbed into the lower part of the tree and picked up the small cat.

"You're shaking," she said, as she put Kismet inside her jacket, partly to keep her warm and partly to protect her while she climbed back down.

▶▶ A cat in China has grown wings. Granny Feng of Xianyang City was amazed to see what started out as two bumps on her cat's back grow into four-inch furry sprouts, like wings, in less than a month in 2007. The wings are likely to have been caused by abnormalities in the cat's genetic make up.

"It's too cold for Kissy here," Zia told Jack when he caught up with her. "And Buster is always tormenting her."

"He can't help it," said Jack, as he scratched the dog's head, both its noses twitching excitedly. "It's what dogs do. And Buster here just has a talent for sniffing out trouble."

"Maybe Kismet could live in my dorm room," suggested Zia. "You'd like that wouldn't you, Kissy?"

The small cat purred from inside Zia's jacket as she tickled its face.

"I bet Mr. Clarkson would like that too," Jack said sarcastically. Mr. Clarkson was the school caretaker and he was very strict about anything that could make a mess of his beautiful showcase—Ripley High. "Cats in dorm rooms are most definitely 'bad show'." Jack tried to mimic Mr. Clarkson's British accent as he delivered the caretaker's catchphrase.

"You're not bad show, are you?" Zia asked the cat. "Pff, what's that?" She waved a hand in front of her face as something flew straight at her head. "It won't leave me alone!" She started to run in circles as the flying thing kept up with her.

"Stay still," suggested Jack. "It's some sort of fly."

"A really annoying one," Zia told him. She zipped her jacket higher to protect Kismet, who was still tucked inside.

"I'll get it," Jack offered, trying to catch the insect that cleverly kept avoiding his grasp. He stopped, thinking he heard laughter, and raised his hand to silence Zia, but she was still trying to lose the fly.

"Ha-ha-ha, something 'bugging' you, Z?" Max stepped out from behind a tree, his face crinkled with laughter.

▸▸ Scientists at Harvard University have created a life-size robotic fly. Weighing only 0.002 ounces with a wingspan of just over an inch, it is hoped that the mechanical insects might one day be used as spies, or for detecting dangerous chemicals.

▸▸ The US military have developed a way to manipulate real flying beetles using wireless control.

"Is that fly something to do with you?" Jack asked.

"Maybe ..." Max replied with a wry smile, holding what looked suspiciously like a remote control in his hand.

"I should have known," said Jack, not sure if he should be frustrated with Max or impressed by him.

"I told you it was something annoying," said Zia.

"Why don't you direct it away from Zia?" asked Jack.

"It's a robotic homing fly," Max explained. "I set it to track you, Jack, but as always, when something electronic gets near Zia, anything can happen!"

Zia walked calmly, but rather crossly, over to them.

"Thanks, Max," she said.

"Wait, where's my—" Max was about to ask what had happened to his fly, but his attention was drawn to the strange sounds coming from Zia's jacket—Kismet was gnawing on the robotic fly, which was still buzzing away pathetically.

"Hey!" he complained prying the chewed robot away from the cat.

"She can't help it," said Zia, thinking of Jack's earlier defence of Buster. "It's what cats do."

Max was about to object when his R-phone buzzed, as did Zia's and Jack's.

"It's a Museum Club message," Jack announced. "Mr. Cain needs us at the RBI base straight away. He says we might be terrified, but he's spelled it wrong." The RBI was secret within Ripley High; the agents were the only students who knew of its existence. In order to keep his messages calling the members to come together secret, Mr. Cain would code them as "Museum Club." However, he was usually unable to resist sending them a clue as to

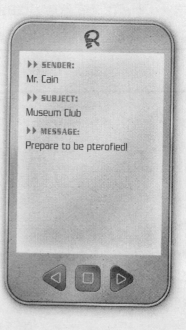

▶▶ SENDER:
Mr. Cain

▶▶ SUBJECT:
Museum Club

▶▶ MESSAGE:
Prepare to be pterofied!

what their latest mission would be.

The three agents quickly left the menagerie and headed back to the school.

"Wait!" said Zia, as they walked through the large front doors of the Ripley High building that had, at one time, been a private house. "I have to go and drop ... something off at my room." She was going to say Kismet, as the winged cat was still hidden inside her jacket, but she was worried that she might be overheard.

"You'd better be quick then," said Jack. "We'll cover for you with Mr. C."

Zia nodded her thanks to the boys, when a loud voice stopped all three of them.

"You three! Stop right there. This time, I know you're up to no good," boomed Mr. Clarkson.

2

Crazy Creature

"What could you possibly mean, Sir?" asked Max, putting on his most innocent-looking face, which for Max was not very innocent at all.

"I can smell something," said Mr. Clarkson, his nose twitching like one of Buster's. "Something that smells like bad show." He moved closer to the agents, sniffing. "And that bad show smells like ... cat!"

The caretaker shouted the last word as the boys moved together, blocking Zia. She didn't need Kobe's telepathic tendencies to know what they were doing. Quickly, she bent down and unzipped her jacket, letting Kismet out and gently touching the cat to let her know she should run off and play, which is exactly what she did.

"What are you doing?" Mr. Clarkson asked, seeing Zia bending down.

"Just tying my shoelace, Sir," said Zia. She stood back up to see Kismet run down the hall behind Mr. Clarkson, her wings flapping. After a moment, she rose off the floor into the air.

"Cat?" asked Max. "There's no such thing!"

Jack and Zia winced at Max's silly response. Max was very used to trying to talk himself out of trouble, although he tended to talk himself into more trouble than he got out of. He seemed to realize he had said the wrong thing, too.

"Er, I mean—"

"What he means," Jack took over, "is that we've just been to the menagerie, and there are lots of cats there."

"Yes," said Max, recovering and seeing an opportunity. "Mr. Clarkson, I'm very impressed. You must really have such an amazing sense of smell that you picked up on the cats in the menagerie. Can you smell the monkeys, too?"

"I didn't think you liked animals," Mr. Clarkson said to Max, not quite ready to believe his story. "What monkeys were you with?"

"I love animals!" Max insisted, looking hurt. "And I love monkeys! Especially that ... that gorilla ... um, the one who speaks in sign language ... I love ... um ..."

▶▶ Koko the gorilla has worked with researchers at the Gorilla Foundation in California for over 30 years. She now knows over 1,000 different expressions in sign language. In fact many great apes have been taught sign language, and they have even been known to teach each other.

"Koko," Jack added, helpfully.

"Yes, Koko," said Max. "I love Koko."

"Hmmm," said Mr. Clarkson, suspiciously. "What was that?" A shout came from down the hall. Zia caught Jack's eye as they saw what had happened. Kismet, in her flight along a corridor, had come across some other Ripley High students, who weren't expecting to see a winged cat in mid-air.

"Uh, we have to go, Sir," said Jack, pulling the other two with him.

Mr. Clarkson, however, didn't really notice. Instantly, he had turned off and was following the sound of whatever 'bad show' was disrupting his quiet corridor.

"What about Kismet?" said Zia in a worried whisper. "We can't just leave her. What if Mr. Clarkson finds her?"

"I'd worry more about Mr. Clarkson finding out you brought her here," said Max as they rushed off.

"Did you mean to spell terrified wrong?"

When Jack, Max, and Zia arrived at the RBI base, Li was quizzing Mr. Cain on the riddle he had sent with their Museum Club message.

"I didn't," said Mr. Cain with a mysterious smile.

"He spelled it as in pterosaur," explained Kate. "Pterofied?"

"That's a very bad joke, Sir," said Alek. "And what has a flying reptile got to do with our next mission?"

"I thought it was quite clever," their teacher replied, smiling. "RIPLEY?" he called.

The holographic head of Robert Ripley appeared above the desk and greeted them all.

"I told him it was a bad joke too," said RIPLEY.

"I really thought that perhaps my English wasn't as good as I imagined," said Alek.

"So what is our mission?" asked Kobe.

"Something strange has been seen in the skies over London," said RIPLEY. "It could be a giant bird, a really large bat, or some sort of flying reptile." He looked at Jack as he said the last bit, knowing Jack was the animal expert.

The large screen behind RIPLEY flashed

into life and a video started to play. A very shaky image of the sky came into view. Then a building, then a statue, then back to the sky.

"Why do people always film things on their phones?" asked Max, annoyed at the jumpy footage.

"Because people don't tend to carry professional video equipment around with them," Jack mocked.

"Well, they should," said Max.

"Ssh, what's that sound?" asked Li, focusing on the high-pitched noise that was coming from the screen.

"It's probably the phone," said Max.

Mr. Cain shot Max a stern look, which silenced him immediately. "Li? What is it that you can hear?" he asked. Li was the RBI's music and sound expert, and if she had heard something it might be important.

"Whoa!" shouted Max, breaking Li's concentration as he watched something moving on the screen.

"Crikey, what was that thing?" asked Jack.

A blurry image had shot across the scene. It was moving very fast, and it was in the air. Mr. Cain rewound the footage a fraction and paused it as the flying thing appeared

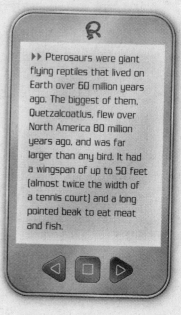

▶▶ Pterosaurs were giant flying reptiles that lived on Earth over 60 million years ago. The biggest of them, Quetzalcoatlus, flew over North America 80 million years ago, and was far larger than any bird. It had a wingspan of up to 50 feet (almost twice the width of a tennis court) and a long pointed beak to eat meat and fish.

on the screen. The agents all crowded round the frozen image, trying to get a better look at what it was.

"I don't think that's any sort of bird," said Jack. "It's just too big."

"But it has wings," said Zia, pointing out the shape of the creature's wings.

"Perhaps it is a pterosaur, like Mr. Cain thought."

"Are those some sort of feathers?" asked Kobe, indicating an orangey section of what looked like a wing.

"It looks like fire to me," said Alek.

"It certainly could be some sort of energy source," Max added. "This really blurry bit," Max felt he had to explain as the whole image was pretty blurry, "could be a heat haze."

"Maybe it's a robot?" said Zia.

Mr. Cain nodded his approval at the agents' observations. He pressed "play" and the creature again whizzed across the sky, the strange noise growing louder and then fainter as the fuzzy image moved in and out of view.

"Now Li, what do you think about that noise?" he asked.

"At first I thought it might be some sort of car engine," she said, "but it sounds smaller and more metallic, almost like a whirring. It actually sounds a bit like a vacuum cleaner!"

"It really could be that the sound has distorted through the recording," Max offered, building on his earlier point.

"You're right, it could," said Mr. Cain. "That's why Li," he turned toward her, "you are going on this mission to see if you can find out any more by hearing the noise in person. Because we still don't know if this thing is robotic or biological, your ability to identify sounds will be really useful."

"And if it turns out to be a giant bat, Li can talk to it in sonar!" Max added helpfully.

"You're going too, Max," said Mr. Cain. "If this is some sort of robot, you're the best person to look into that."

"But what if it is some sort of giant, prehistoric creature—like a pterosaur?" asked Jack.

"Then hopefully you'll be there to find out," said Mr. Cain. "You, Jack, are going to be the third agent on the team."

"The person who shot this video was on their way to work," continued Mr. Cain.

"And still half-asleep, by the looks of it," grumbled Max, objecting again to the quality of the footage.

"And it just so happens that they work in the Ripley's museum in London," said Mr. Cain, ignoring him. "The team will be based there while they are investigating."

3

Supersonic Sensors

Jack, Max, and Li, the three agents selected for the mission, went next door to Dr. Maxwell's lab. Dr. Maxwell was the only other teacher who knew about the RBI. As their resident gadget man and "mad professor" (according to most of the agents), Dr. Maxwell had a second lab alongside his regular science classroom in the futuristic basement of the building that was home to the RBI base.

"Oh Max, I'm glad you're here," said Dr. Maxwell. "I've been having real trouble with level six of one of those games you lent me: Warriors of Fire."

"Let me guess," said Max. "You can't get into the fortress because the vicious guard dog keeps ripping your avatar to pieces?"

"Yes!" Dr. Maxwell exclaimed. "How did you know? You've not been using one of those spying devices on me again, have you?"

"I had trouble at that part too, for a couple of minutes," said Max, coolly. "You have to try to tickle the dog's tummy."

"Well, I never would have thought of that!" said the professor, laughing. "That's the sort of advice I would have expected to get from Jack here."

"Yawn," said Li. As the RBI's computer expert, Max spent a lot of time in Dr. Maxwell's lab, and the two had become quite good friends, especially since Max had discovered that his professor loved computer games almost as much as he did.

"Ah, yes, sorry," said Dr. Maxwell. "Back to work."

He pulled out some strange devices that looked like thick felt-tip pens. There were three of them.

▶▶ In 2005, a 28-year-old man collapsed and died after playing the online multiplayer game Starcraft for 50 hours continuously at an internet café in Taegu, South Korea. He only took short toilet breaks, and it is thought that he died from heart failure due to exhaustion.

"Pens?" asked Li.

"No, they may look like pens, but they are my supersonic sensors," he explained. "They will use sound waves in the air to tell you when the creature you are tracking comes within range."

"What's their range?" asked Li.

"Whatever you set it to be," said Dr. Maxwell. "You set the three sensors up in different parts of London and switch them on. They create laser-like lines linking with the others, which make a triangle. Anything within that triangle is in range."

"Ah, I see," said Li.

Dr. Maxwell handed her a device that looked a bit like her R-phone but with a larger screen.

"The map will appear on here," he told her.

"Won't it just track everything and everyone in London that's inside the triangle?" asked

Jack. "How will it know to look for our flying thing?"

"Well, you'll have to make sure you get the sensors as high as possible," the professor told them. "That way it will only track things in the sky. Try to find the tallest buildings you can, and place the sensors there. Then they won't be high enough to track aircraft, but the creature we are looking for should be the only thing in the air at that height and size."

The agents nodded and Max put the tracking device into his bag.

"Shall we go to see Miss Burrows now?" asked Li. Miss Burrows was the team's geography and history teacher and although she didn't know that the RBI existed, the agents found that it was always worth speaking to her before a mission. Without knowing it, Miss Burrows helped them research the area they would be visiting.

"You two go ahead," said Max. "I'm going to

stay here and try to fix my fly."

"Your what?" asked Li, as Max pulled the chewed mechanical insect out of his pocket.

"Zia's cat tried to eat it," Max said sadly, as he put the still buzzing fly on the table.

"Oh well, it's not the end of the world," said Dr. Maxwell encouragingly. "I'm sure you'll be able to mend it."

Max started to collect the things he would need, as Jack and Li left the lab.

"Hold it right there," Mr. Cain called after the two agents as they headed toward the staircase out of the secret RBI base. They turned to face their teacher.

"We're about to go see Miss Burrows," Li told him.

"Well, you might be, but Jack's not."

"Why not?" asked Jack, looking alarmed.

"Because you have to help Zia."

"Help Zia with what?" asked Jack.

"Mr. Clarkson has had to go deal with a group of screaming second-year girls," Mr. Cain explained. "Apparently, they were being terrorized by a flying cat."

Jack felt his face flush with guilt.

"I'm sure it's nothing to do with you or Zia," said Mr. Cain, although from his tone and the look on his face Jack could see that his teacher

knew it had everything to do with him and Zia. "However, you are our resident animal expert, and I know Zia is particularly fond of Kismet the winged cat, so I thought the pair of you would be only too glad to help."

"Of course, Mr. C," Jack nodded.

"But that's not fair," said Li, trying to stand up for her friend. "Jack needs to come see Miss—"

Jack threw her a sideways look knowing that Kismet's escape was partly his fault anyway. "It's fine, Li," he said. "You go see Miss Burrows and I'll find out what she told you later."

"Good," said Mr. Cain. "If that's settled, Jack, you can find Zia and the cat in the cafeteria."

Jack winced as he imagined the chaos that Kismet could have caused flying around."

4

Believe It or Not!

"Look, a London bus!" said Max, pointing as a large red double-decker, the sort that the city is famous for, drove past. It was closely followed by a black taxi, which was beeping its horn at the bus.

"It's so exciting here," said Jack. "It's really loud and busy."

"It reminds me a bit of home," said Li, looking at the enormous buildings that rose up on either side of the road, making the street seem narrower. She had grown up in Beijing and was much more used to the hustle and bustle of city life than Jack.

"But how did we manage to hear the noise that the creature made so loudly on the video?" Jack asked, thinking to himself that London had been much quieter on the video.

"Mornings are often quieter, before all the tourists arrive," Li told him.

"Wow, look at that building," said Max, pointing to a large structure with ornate detailing around the windows and columns guarding the entrance. The huge building covered a whole block. As the agents turned a corner, they were met with a giant Ripley's Believe It or Not! sign.

"It looks like that's where the museum is, then," said Jack.

They walked closer to the entrance. Loud music was blaring from speakers and a huge inflatable of the tallest man in the world leaned out from one of the doors.

"It's like a party in there," said Li, looking at the invitingly bright lights.

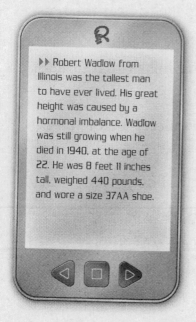

▶▶ Robert Wadlow from Illinois was the tallest man to have ever lived. His great height was caused by a hormonal imbalance. Wadlow was still growing when he died in 1940, at the age of 22. He was 8 feet 11 inches tall, weighed 440 pounds, and wore a size 37AA shoe.

"Then why don't you come and join in?" asked a girl in a red "Ripley's" polo shirt, as she stepped outside and greeted the agents.

"I think we just might," said Max, breaking into a huge grin.

"We're here from the RBI," Jack told her.

"Oh, my goodness!" she said, her enthusiasm obvious. "You're from the RBI? I'm so excited! Of course, we were told you would be coming, and I've been expecting you, but I can't believe you're actually here! I'm Abby." She held her hand out to introduce herself.

"I'm Jack," he shook her hand, "and this is Li and—"

"I'm Max," Max interrupted, leaping in front of Jack to shake Abby's hand.

"Are you here about the flying thing?" Abby asked.

"Yes, that's right," Li nodded.

"I saw it," said Abby. "It was really weird. And working here every day, I know weird!"

"Then it's you we need to speak to," Max told her.

"Well, and Sam. He sort of saw it too. Come in and we'll go find him."

The agents followed Abby into the museum entrance and through a door marked "staff only." She bounced as she walked, her long dark hair swinging behind her. The agents followed her down a corridor, up a staircase, and into a staff break room.

"Sam?" Abby called, as they entered the room. A young man with glasses looked up from his computer.

"The RBI is here to speak to us about that flying creature we saw!" Her smile had become even wider, if that was possible.

"Wow, the RBI?" said Sam. "I was just looking at websites to see if there were any reports

of anyone else seeing something like we did. So far I can't find anything!"

Jack walked behind Sam and looked at the computer screen. Sam had been on a Ripley's website that had the local news and lots of unbelievable stories on it too. Jack pointed to an article about a winged cat.

"Wow, I wonder if that's an old story about

Kismet, or if it's another winged cat?" he said, making a note on his R-phone to investigate that story later. Another one caught his eye.

"Police baffled as unbelievable London robberies continue," he read. "Maybe we can solve those too if we've got time!" he said laughing.

Sam turned around to face Jack.

"So, you're really the RBI?" he asked. "I'd heard stories about you, but I didn't think you were real."

"We're real," said Jack. "'Believe it or not!'"

Max shook his head at Jack's joke and turned toward Abby. "So, tell us what happened."

"I was on my way to work," she began, "I had just come out of the station across the road from the museum. I was worried that I was going to be late. Then all of a sudden, there was this terrible noise."

"What did it sound like?" asked Li.

"It was horrible. It sounded like something out of some scary sci-fi horror movie. When I got to work Sam was on the ticket desk so I called for him to run down the road and see if he could still see it."

"I ran outside but there was nothing there really," said Sam. "Just a smoke trail in the air."

"I filmed the whole thing on my phone," added Abby. "Did you see the video I made? Was it useful?"

"It was really good," Max told her. "It gave us loads to go on."

Jack gave Max a quizzical look, remembering how much he had complained about the video when RIPLEY had shown it.

"Oh, I'm so pleased!" said Abby, beaming. "I was worried it might be a bit shaky. My phone is quite new."

"So, have you seen the creature again since?" asked Li. Abby shook her head.

"It must be somewhere around here," said Jack. "It might even have some sort of lair nearby."

"Maybe it was just passing through," suggested Sam. "Perhaps it lives somewhere else?"

"It might," agreed Li. "We should set up the tracking towers."

"We need to find the tallest buildings in London," said Max.

"Ooh, I'll go get you a map," said Abby.

"I'll come with you," Sam offered. "My break's over." He turned to the RBI agents. "If you need anything else, you can find me in the shrunken head room."

"Thanks," said Jack.

"Most people are shocked when I tell them that I'm working with the shrunken heads," Sam laughed.

"Not us," said Li. "We have a shrunken head room at our school."

"Now that's amazing! I'd love to see them some time," Sam said smiling, as he and Abby left the room.

"They're really nice," said Li.

"Abby's pretty," said Max.

"Your video footage was really good, Abby," said Jack, mimicking Max.

"You're just jealous," Max teased. Jack started to protest, but then stopped as Abby came back into the room with a map.

"Let's split up," said Jack. "If we each take a sensor and place it on one of the tallest buildings, it will be faster. We'll decide where to go once we've seen a map. Then we'll meet back here afterward."

The others nodded their agreement.

The three RBI agents met back at the Ripley's museum just as it began to get dark. Max was holding the receiver and the screen showed the triangle formed by the three towers.

"So this triangle covers most of London?" asked Li.

"A good portion of it," Max told her.

"And what's that dot?" asked Li, as a small blip appeared on the screen near one of their sensors.

"That might just be our flying creature," said Max.

5

Mini Madness

"If that's our creature, then it's moving very fast," said Jack, looking at the small dot as it made its way quickly across the illuminated screen.

"We'll need to hurry if we're going to catch it," said Li.

"How far is this on foot?" Max asked Abby. "Can we run there?"

Abby shook her head. "No, it's quite a way."

"Then how will we ever get there?" asked Li.

"Why don't you take the Mini?" suggested Abby. The agents looked at her, confused. "The crystal Mini," she added, pointing to one of the exhibits in the corner of the entrance hall: a Mini Cooper car covered in thousands of crystals. "Minis are great for getting around London. They're so small."

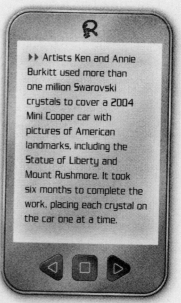

▶▶ Artists Ken and Annie Burkitt used more than one million Swarovski crystals to cover a 2004 Mini Cooper car with pictures of American landmarks, including the Statue of Liberty and Mount Rushmore. It took six months to complete the work, placing each crystal on the car one at a time.

"Okay then, let's hurry," said Jack. "I'll drive."

"The only thing you'll have to worry about is the traffic lights," Abby warned. "There are quite a few around here."

"Leave that to me," said Max, climbing into the passenger seat and pulling a small handheld computer out of his backpack. Soon, the agents were racing through the narrow streets of London in the Mini. Huge buildings loomed on either side of the road and the sidewalks were packed with people. Jack felt quite boxed in as he moved the car through the maze of roads.

"Traffic light!" he yelled, seeing a set of lights ahead that were about to change.

"I'm on it," Max told him. Max's ability to do incredible things with computers meant that he had been able to hack into the London traffic system and control the lights. Every time the agents approached a set of red lights, Max would send a signal to change them to green. At the same time, he set the lights in all the other directions to red, stopping the rest of the traffic until the agents, in their unbelievable

car, were safely past.

"There are going to be some angry people," said Li, as she saw the traffic building up along the roads they passed.

"The creature is heading south!" shouted Max, holding the receiver for the triangulation tracking device and following the small blip that was moving across the screen. He was directing Jack toward it, but it kept moving. Every time the dot changed course, Max called out its new direction and Jack would try to catch up with it.

Jack now took the first turn he could to change their route again.

"It's moving toward the river now," called Max, as the blip moved across the screen until it was traveling along next to the River Thames.

"Hang on," said Jack, wrenching the Mini's steering wheel hard to the left. The car screeched as it turned sharply, almost missing the narrow side street that he was hoping to take.

"Turn right here," suggested Max. Jack did as he was asked, but immediately met cars heading toward them! Horns blared and lights flashed as Jack frantically tried to move the Mini out of the path of the oncoming cars. Li screamed as a large truck cut across their path.

Jack pulled up on to the sidewalk, blasting his own horn to warn the people walking there to move out the way. He found himself heading straight toward a market area and couldn't stop the car before it drove right through a flower stand.

"Sorry!" Jack called out the window, as the stall keeper shook his fist angrily at the Mini. He looked across to see Max clutching a bunch of flowers.

"They just landed in my lap!" he explained in answer to Jack's disapproving look. "I thought I might take them back for Abby."

"Just tell me which direction I should be driving!" Jack told him, annoyed that

Max didn't seem to be taking this very seriously.

"We need to turn right to get to the river. Drive through that outdoor cafe, that would be the quickest way."

Jack did as Max instructed and headed toward the cafe.

"Aim for that table," Max pointed to where a waiter was just delivering some food. "I could really do with a burger!"

Jack pulled the car away from the cafe at the last moment and skidded around it. One waiter dropped the tray he was carrying, more in shock at seeing the crystal-covered car than avoiding it, but other than that no one was disturbed.

"Spoilsport," grumbled Max. "Take that road there. Then you'll need to go left, then left, then right then, oh..." he paused.

"What?" Jack asked.

"It'll be fine," said Max. "So left, left, right, and then left."

Jack took the directions Max gave him. "We still seem too high up for the river," he commented.

"Do we?" asked Max, but his voice sounded as if he already knew that.

Jack turned the final left and gasped at the sight ahead of him.

"Have we gone the wrong way?" he asked.

The car was headed toward a very steep set of stone steps.

"No, I think we're okay," Max said, still sounding very cool, as though he was expecting this.

"What about the steps?" Jack asked.

"We drive down them." Max broke into a huge grin as he made the suggestion. "It's the fastest way," he explained, seeing Jack's

excited look.

"Hang on then," said Jack. "Hold tight!"

In the back seat Li screwed her eyes tightly shut, held on to the seat and placed her feet firmly on the floor, bracing herself for the impact.

As the car bumped down the steps, the agents jostled up and down with it.

"I c-can fee-e-l e-v-ery bone in m-my bod-y-y bump-in-g," said Li, her voice shaking with the car.

The stairs turned a sharp corner and Jack turned the car with it, bumping the Mini down the second half of the stairs. People leaped out of the way with puzzled looks—a Mini driving down a flight of steps wasn't something you see every day in London, and certainly not one covered from front to back in crystals!

At the bottom of the steps, the car drove back on to the road that was running next to the river.

"He's straight in front of us," said Max, noticing that the dot on the screen was very close. Jack speeded up and rocketed along beside the water. They rushed on forward past many of London's bridges.

"We're closing in on it," said Max. "It should be right ahead of us!"

Jack looked up and saw the most famous of London's bridges, Tower Bridge.

"Wait a minute—" said Max. He was looking at the screen, but the dot seemed to have just disappeared. "Where's it gone?"

"Where's what gone?" asked Jack.

"Stop the car," Max told him. He jumped out the passenger door and held the receiver up in the air, hoping that something had blocked the signal, and the dot would reappear.

"It's just gone," he said. "The dot, it's vanished."

Jack took the receiver and looked at it too. There was nothing there.

"The creature has obviously flown out of range," said Li.

"It must have," agreed Max, still confused.

"I was driving my best," Jack told them, "but I just don't see how we can catch the creature if it's flying and we're trying to drive along busy London streets."

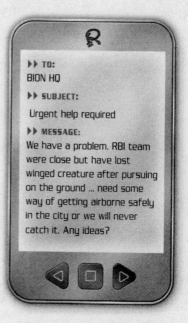

▶▶ TO:
BION HQ

▶▶ SUBJECT:
Urgent help required

▶▶ MESSAGE:
We have a problem. RBI team were close but have lost winged creature after pursuing on the ground ... need some way of getting airborne safely in the city or we will never catch it. Any ideas?

"I think we should call BION Island for help," Jack suggested.

"Good idea," said Li. "Someone there will be able to think of something."

6

Squirrel Suits

The following morning, the agents arrived back at the Ripley's museum.

"RIPLEY said that he would be sending something to help us," Jack told the others.

"I wonder what he has thought up," said Li.

The agents were greeted by Abby, who was her normal cheery self.

"There's someone here to see you," she told them.

"Wow, RIPLEY must have worked out something really quickly," said Li, amazed.

Abby took the agents into the museum to an area with lots of shelves that were stacked high with boxes, all labeled with what was inside them.

"These are all things that Mr. Ripley found on his travels," Abby explained, as they made their way through the towering shelves.

"I don't think Rip found *him*," said Max, pointing at the figure leaning halfway inside one of the boxes, looking for something.

"It's Dr. Maxwell," giggled Li, as their professor emerged from the box.

"I heard you could use some help," he said, "so I flew in overnight."

"Aren't you tired?" asked Li.

"No, if I don't get much sleep it's not the end of the world for me," he told them. "I'm used to staying up all night and working on inventions. Which reminds me ..." he started digging around in one of the boxes again. "I brought you these!" He pulled out what looked like ski suits.

"What are they?" asked Max.

"They're called 'squirrel suits', or 'wingsuits'," explained Dr. Maxwell. "They are suits that can also act as parachutes. They have material sewn between the legs and under the arms." He stretched the suit out so the agents could see the extra material. "With these, you can jump off high buildings. The extra material will act as a parachute to slow your fall, but will also trap air and create lift, allowing you to travel farther."

"They sound great," said Max. "But can we walk in them? Won't we trip over, as if our legs are tied together?"

"You shouldn't," said Dr. Maxwell. "Why don't you try them on?"

The agents put on the suits. Li looked at herself in a big mirror, a broken pane from

▶▶ In April 2007, American daredevil Jeb Corliss flew in a wingsuit under the giant arm of the Jesus Christ statue that overlooks Rio de Janeiro, Brazil. He passed about three feet from the 120-foot structure at high speed, after jumping from a plane at a height of nearly 15,000 feet.

the mirror maze that was being stored there.

"I look like a huge marshmallow," she complained as the trick glass distorted her shape. She turned to Dr. Maxwell. "One day, I hope you're going to come to me with an amazing invention that is also fashionable and won't make me look so silly."

"Fashion's not really my thing, I'm afraid, Li," said Dr. Maxwell.

"We inventors have much more important things to worry about than what the latest trend is," added Max.

Li looked at Dr. Maxwell with his huge bushy hair and Max who always wore the same overalls, thinking to herself that it was quite obvious that neither of them worried too much about how they looked.

While the others were discussing fashion, or lack of fashion, Jack was taking some time to look at the labels of the things on the shelves.

"Tribal warrior mask, bubblegum bird,

fossilized dinosaur egg, tooth tattoos," he read out the tags that were tied to the objects or brown boxes that lined the shelves all around him.

In between two large brown boxes, Jack saw a flash of color: something red and yellow peeped out at him. He decided that it was his duty as an RBI agent to investigate. Standing on tiptoe, he reached in behind the boxes. His hand grabbed something metallic and he pulled it out toward him. It was an intricately designed tin, very similar to four other tins that were stored in the secret RBI base back at Ripley High. Those tins had all been found by agents while on missions. In the Florida Everglades, Kobe had discovered an artifact that had once belonged to Robert Ripley and had gone missing from Ripley High. When they brought it back to BION Island, the artifact had launched them on an amazing quest. Rip had hidden special artifacts all around the

world and left clues to help those who followed him find the treasures. So far, every clue the agents had found had been in a red and yellow tin, just like the one Jack was now holding in his hand. He walked back to Dr. Maxwell and the other agents with his discovery.

"It's a clue tin," said Li, recognizing it at once. "Have you opened it?"

Jack shook his head. There was a label on the tin, similar to the ones on the other boxes, but instead of having a description of what was inside, it had a message on it: "To those who follow me."

"That looks like Rip's writing," said Li.

Jack looked around for Abby. The museum staff member was filing more exhibits two rows along.

"Where did this come from?" he asked her.

"I don't know," she admitted. "When the museum opened we received artifacts from lots of the other museums, and this must have come in with them.

"Can we open it?" asked Max.

"Of course," said Abby. "You're RBI agents— nothing here is off limits to you!"

Jack gently worked the lid off the tin and tipped its contents out into Li's hands.

"It's a book," she said, slightly puzzled. The book was a biography of a 1920s explorer.

"Eugh, it's a history book," complained Max. "How can this be a useful clue? Are there any pictures, at least?"

"I think it's important," said Li. "It's in a clue tin, and the message says that it's for those who follow Rip. That's the RBI—that's us! I'm going to contact Kate. She'll love it, and I bet she'll find something in there that will finally lead us to that hidden artifact."

"Before you do that, I still have something else to show you," said Dr. Maxwell.

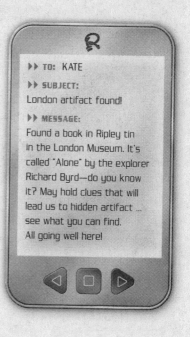

▶▶ **TO:** KATE

▶▶ **SUBJECT:**
London artifact found!

▶▶ **MESSAGE:**
Found a book in Ripley tin in the London Museum. It's called "Alone" by the explorer Richard Byrd—do you know it? May hold clues that will lead us to hidden artifact ... see what you can find. All going well here!

He was holding a hook attached to a long rope.

"It's a grappling hook," said Jack. "I've used those before on trips into the outback with my dad."

"Ah, but this isn't just any grappling hook," said Dr. Maxwell. "It's a magnetic grappling hook."

"Like in Treasures of the Amazon?" asked Max, referring to one of his computer games.

"Exactly like that," said Dr. Maxwell.

"Well then, I've used one of those heaps of times." Max turned to the others. "It works in pretty much the same way as regular grappling hooks. You throw the hook and it latches on to something. But the magnet means that it will attach itself to metal much more easily. And see this button?" he pointed to a small button at the end of the rope. "If you press this, the magnet and the hook let go. It's really useful if you've used the hook to swing across a fiery canyon on to a bridge and need to get your hook back."

"I doubt there'll be much swinging across canyons onto bridges," said Li. She couldn't believe the way Max thought that if he'd done something in a computer game it meant that he'd really done it.

"But it will be useful for helping you get to

the top of high things so that you can jump off them in your wingsuits," said Dr. Maxwell. "I suggest that you wait until tonight and then find some good, high spots to start on."

"Why should we wait till tonight?" asked Max.

"Every sighting RIPLEY had cataloged for this creature is at night, or early in the morning," said Dr. Maxwell. "Also it will be much easier for you to fly around at night without everyone in London noticing you and wondering what's going on! Teenagers in flying suits aren't an everyday sight, you know!"

"We know that something strange happened near Tower Bridge," Max reminded the others. "I think we should each take up a position near there. I'm sure it has something to do with the flying creature."

The other agents agreed.

7

Fantastic Flights

As night fell, the agents were all in position. Li was waiting on the huge clock that rang the hour for the British Houses of Parliament. Big Ben had already chimed once and Li, with her supersensitive hearing, wished that she had chosen a quieter location.

When she heard a strange whirring sound, at first she wondered if it was the ringing in her ears that had been caused by the bell, but then she realized that she had heard this sound before, in a video. It was the noise that Abby's camera phone had recorded when the flying creature had appeared!

As the sound grew louder, Li leaped from the clock tower, hoping to catch up with whatever was making the strange noise. Her suit caught the air and she soared like a bird into the night sky, surrounded by the lights from the city's amazing buildings.

Li was just getting used to the feeling when the creature appeared to her left. It was huge! It didn't look like any sort of bird or animal she had ever seen. Using the radio in her RBI wingsuit, she radioed to the other two agents that she had seen the creature and was chasing it.

"Jack, you really have to see this!" she exclaimed. "It's like nothing I've ever seen before. I just hope that you know what sort of animal it is."

"Should I move toward you?" Jack asked. He was waiting on the London Eye, the massive wheel on the bank of the River Thames that gave passengers a bird's eye view of London.

"No, I'll try to bring it to you," Li told him. As soon as she said it though, the creature turned away and headed back toward the city. Li chased after it, but it speeded up, as if it knew it was being followed and was trying to lose its shadow.

As Li followed the creature through the urban jungle of London town, she realized that she was beginning to lose height. The wingsuit had allowed her to travel quite a distance, but gravity was pulling her back down to earth. As best she could, Li herded the creature back through the maze of skyscrapers and monuments to the river. They were just about to pass the London Eye as she landed on the ground beside the water.

"It's all yours, Jack," she said over the microphone.

"I've got it," said Jack as he swooped off the big wheel and into the air. "We're heading toward you, Max."

The creature flew straight along the river now, rising to fly over the bridges. Jack did his best to keep up, remembering everything he knew about the way birds and bats moved to help him maintain height. He was also racking his brain to think of anything he knew about flying creatures to help explain what this thing could be. A couple of times, Jack thought he saw what looked like fire surrounding the creature's wings, lighting up the dark sky around it. He thought about fiery mythical creatures, like the phoenix and dragons that breathed fire, and wondered if whatever this was could be the basis for some of those stories. Jack had heard about animals that had lived for millions of years undiscovered in some of the world's rainforests; perhaps this was one of those. However, it still didn't explain what it was doing in a big city.

The creature began to duck under bridges as well as flying over them, and Jack followed it. It wasn't until after he had flown under the second bridge that he realized what was happening. The flying thing knew it was being followed and knew how his suit worked. Having lowered himself almost to water level to go under the last bridge, Jack wasn't able to raise himself again to fly over the next one.

"He's all yours, Max," said Jack, seeing Tower

Bridge not too far in front of him.

"Got it," said Max.

Jack used the little height he had left to direct himself to the edge of the water. He touched down in the middle of the terrace of an expensive-looking restaurant and diners looked up from their plates in amazement as he swooped in. Jack waved to let them know

everything was all right and left as soon as he could.

As soon as he heard Jack's message, Max leaped off from his position on Tower Bridge. He saw the creature a little way down the river, quite low to the water, and thought about how he would get to it before it passed under the bridge. He knew the extra material in his suit worked like a parachute and slowed the speed at which he would fly. So, if he pulled his arms in and kept his legs together, he would simply fall. Max did just that; he fell toward the ground like a missile, only opening up the suit when the water seemed dangerously close.

As he did so, Max heard a loud ripping sound. He looked to the side and saw that the material in his suit had torn. The speed at which he had been falling had been so great that when he opened the wings the pressure

of the air had ripped through them. There was now nothing to slow his fall and he was heading fast, much too fast, toward the black, dark water that lay only a short distance below him.

8

Robofly Returns

Max's arms and legs thrashed wildly as he panicked, seeing the hard sheet of water coming ever closer. He screwed his eyes shut, ready for the impact of his body hitting the river, which at this speed would have the same effect as hitting a brick wall; but instead, he felt himself being lifted gently back into the air.

Max looked up and saw a black shape looming above him in the darkness. He went back to waving his arms around and screaming. He did not want to be taken back to this huge, hideous bird's lair for supper! Fire erupted around him, Max tried to make his shouts even louder, calling for help from anyone who could possibly hear him.

On the river in front of them, Max saw a boat taking the city's garbage to a dump. He thought that if only he could free himself he could land on the boat and let it carry him to safety. He shook and squirmed as much as he possibly could, still screaming for someone to rescue him. The boat got nearer and Max felt himself being lowered toward it. He wriggled even more and felt the thing's grip on him loosen.

As he finally freed himself and fell on to the boat, Max thought that he heard a voice. He looked around and saw the creature flying away.

Max shivered at the thought of what the creature might have done to him had he let it carry him off.

"Max, up here!" he heard Li's voice from a bridge a little way down the river and looked through the darkness to see the other two RBI agents waving RBI-issue strobe lights and calling to him. Not wanting the others to think that he had been scared, Max smiled in case they could see him through the darkness, pretending that everything was fine and unhooked his grappling hook from where it had been stowed in his suit.

He skillfully swung the hook up toward the bridge, pressing the button that would magnetize the hook. It stuck fast to the iron

bridge and Max was able to swing himself up and over the side.

Once he had climbed to safety he pressed the button again, releasing the hook and reeling the whole thing in.

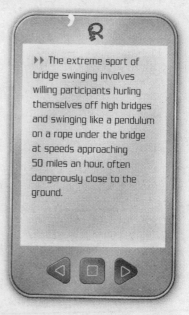

The extreme sport of bridge swinging involves willing participants hurling themselves off high bridges and swinging like a pendulum on a rope under the bridge at speeds approaching 50 miles an hour, often dangerously close to the ground.

"I told you we'd need to swing on to bridges," he told Li.

"We were so worried," she told him, ignoring his comment. "We saw that creature grab you and thought it was going to carry you away."

"It would have, if I hadn't kept so cool and made it release me," Max shrugged.

"Yeah, you were cool, alright," Jack smirked. He waved his arms about and jumped from leg to leg. "Someone save me!" he yelled in an imitation of Max. "What were you doing, diving off that bridge without using your suit properly?" he asked. Jack had been worried about his best friend and now Max was safe, Jack was angry at how silly he had been.

"I thought it would be faster," said Max.

Jack tried to calm himself, realizing that there was no point getting annoyed with Max; they all knew how stubborn and reckless he could be.

"It looked more like the creature rescued you," Jack laughed. "If you'd hit that water at that speed, you'd have been a goner."

Max gulped. He knew Jack was right, but he didn't really want to admit his mistake.

The agents ran to their car and made their way back to the Ripley's museum where Abby ran up to them with news.

"There's been another robbery," she told them. "The newspapers are reporting that the flying creature is behind them."

"It couldn't have been," said Jack. "The creature was busy rescuing Max."

"It didn't rescue me," said Max, sensing everyone's eyes on him and feeling a bit silly. "It tried to take me to its lair."

"It's a shame it couldn't rescue us from the smell," said Li. "Phew!"

"It's not my fault!" said Max. "It was the garbage boat I landed on!"

"Did you find the creature's lair?" asked Dr. Maxwell, changing the subject.

"No," Jack replied. "It got away."

"I still think it's some sort of prehistoric creature, maybe a pterosaur," said Jack. "But how on earth could such a creature commit robberies? That's ridiculous! None of this makes any sense."

"Well that's what they're saying," said Abby.

"We need to find that creature even more now," said Li.

"But how can we? We have no idea where it went," said Jack. He looked at the map linked to the supersonic sensors. "The creature doesn't even seem to be in the area we can track now."

"We can still track it," said Max. He pulled his R-phone out of his pocket. After pressing a few buttons a map came up, similar to the one they had used to track the creature earlier.

"What's that?" asked Li.

"When the creature grabbed me, I put a tracker on him," Max explained. "Something small that will stay with him and allow us to follow him."

"Don't tell me you stuck robofly on him?" laughed Jack.

"Yes, I did," said Max. The fly that Jack had tormented Zia with back at Ripley High was now tracking the creature and reporting its location back to Max.

"You're a genius," Jack smiled.

9

Towers and Terrors

"Robofly is beeping!" shouted Li, pointing at Max's R-phone, which was vibrating and making loud noises to alert them.

"It's at Tower Bridge again," said Max.

The three RBI agents rushed to the bridge, once again driving the crystal-covered Mini at top speed through the streets of London.

When they arrived at Tower Bridge, the agents pulled out their magnetic grappling hooks and started to climb up the side of one of the towers. Robofly's signal was telling them that they were getting close. Max swung himself toward one of the tower windows, which was ajar, but his magnetic hook just missed.

"Max," shouted Li in alarm as she saw her friend falling. She reached out for him, but he had already passed her.

As he began to fall he threw his hook upward again, and felt it snag on something.

A yell from above him told him that it was Jack!

"Careful," said Jack once Max appeared beside him, having reeled himself up again. "That was very nearly my foot you hooked on to."

Max swung his hook more carefully this time through the tower window and followed it inside.

"Wow, check this out!" he called back to the others.

Jack and Li appeared through the open window and took in the scene that had amazed Max. It was a small room and every wall was covered in posters. Some were from films, some were comic book pictures, and others looked as if they were drawn by hand. All the posters were of superheroes. The floor was littered with comics, all with pictures of heroes on the cover, flying through the air or ready to fight the villain.

▶▶ One of the most expensive comics in the world, Action Comics No. 1, introduced Superman for the first time in 1938. A copy was sold for $195,000 in 2004.

▶▶ In 2009, a collection of 3,000 comic books worth over $1 million was discovered in a house that sold for just $65,000 in St. Louis, Missouri, USA!

"This is amazing," said Max. "Some of these comics are really rare and hard to get hold of."

In the corner of the room stood two dummies, like those that display clothes in menswear shops. One of them was wearing a suit. It looked like somebody's homemade version of a comic book superhero suit: it had a headpiece and mask, with large goggles attached to it. Max felt sure he had seen the mask somewhere before. Strapped on to the suit was a huge pair of collapsible fiberglass wings. They spanned almost half the length of the room and had something else attached to them. As the agents moved closer, they saw that each wing had a mini gas turbine stuck to the fiberglass.

"I thought I saw fire," said Jack. "Would you believe it! Our creature is a person who appears

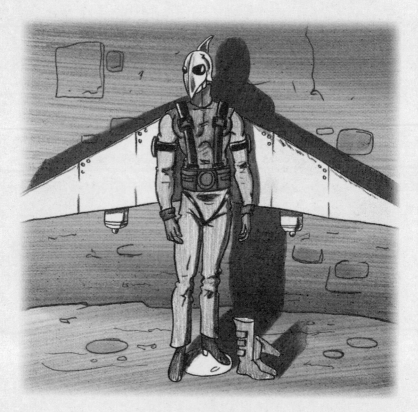

to be wearing an extraordinary flying suit."

"It's a pretty amazing flying suit," added Max. "I wish I'd invented one like this. Those wings are huge, yet it looks like they can collapse to be really small. That must be how he gets them in and out of the room."

"I wonder why the second dummy isn't wearing a suit?" asked Jack.

Before anyone could answer Li held up a hand to silence them, she had heard something.

"Wait, what's that?" asked Li, turning her head to the side so that her incredible hearing could pick out the noise she was listening for. "It sounds like someone running up stone steps." She pointed in the direction the sound was coming from and the agents saw a small door. They all went through it to find a staircase rising up to the top of the tower. The agents quickly ran up it, when an alarm sounded.

"Where is that coming from?" asked Li, clasping her hands over her ears.

"I'd say over there," said Max, as he exited the stairway on to the roof. He pointed to the roof of the building opposite: the Tower of London. As they looked, the other agents saw people on the roof of the tower, wearing ski masks to hide their faces. Lights were flashing and sirens were wailing all around them.

"They must be the thieves," said Li.

The thieves were waving and pointing at something in the sky. It was the person in the flying suit—probably the one who had been running up the stairs ahead of them.

"Stop, thieves!" he shouted, loud enough for the agents on the nearby bridge tower to hear.

The thieves looked petrified by the huge winged creature that had appeared in the sky above them.

They panicked and tried to run away, but in their confusion kept crashing into each other.

They were already on the roof and had nowhere else to go.

"You are surrounded. Throw down your weapons and surrender," boomed the birdman.

The thieves immediately did as they were told, dropping their weapons and bags to the floor. Stolen jewels spilled out all over the roof and glinted in the light that the birdman's flaming burners were shining down on to the scene.

The RBI agents watched from the top of Tower Bridge as the man in the wingsuit slowly moved closer and closer to the cowering thieves.

Sirens approached growing louder and louder.

"The police are here," said Li.

Moments later police ran onto the roof and handcuffed the thieves.

"He really did it," said Max, impressed. "He really stopped the robbery."

10

Birdman

The RBI agents ran as quickly as they could down from the tower and over to the growing chaos around the Tower of London.

Some media vans with journalists and photographers had arrived and everyone was crowding around the police and the thieves. The RBI agents weren't interested in this. They looked around but couldn't see the man in the suit anywhere.

"This way," said Li hearing a noise that she instantly recognized as the suit's engines cooling down. The others followed Li as she ran into a dark alleyway, where they all came face to face with the man in the suit.

"You're amazing!" said Max, his voice full of admiration as they approached the man. "I wish I had a suit as good as yours. How did you make it? Is it difficult to fly? How does it work?"

The man answered all of Max's questions and then the agents interviewed him for the database to find out who he was and what he was doing. He told them his name was Marc Powell and he was a bridge operator at Tower Bridge. It was his job to raise the bridge to let ships pass through. He had always been a huge fan of superheroes and comic books, and the tower operator's room seemed like the perfect base for a superhero. Marc was also really good with electronics. As a trained engineer, part of his role was to make sure all the historical

mechanisms on the bridge kept working. In his spare time, he had decided to make his dream come true and create a superhero outfit for himself. All good superheroes needed to fly and so he had found a way to give himself jet-powered wings that would lift him into the air.

After hearing about the robberies that were

happening throughout London, he had decided that he could really be of help and that this was the ideal time to launch his superhero, "Birdman." However, it all went wrong when people started to think that he was behind the robberies. He was desperate to find the real villains and to clear his name.

▶▶ Superbarrio is a real life South American superhero. The mystery figure, who dresses in a tight red costume, cape, and wrestling mask, has stood up for the rights of the poor and the homeless in Mexico for over a decade. He does not use violence, but organizes protests and petitions instead.

"But you could have been killed," said Li, amazed at the man's bravery.

"I just wanted to help people," he told them. "I had made this amazing suit and it was just sitting there."

Jack explained about the RBI and the Ripley's database. "You can certainly help us! You and your suit are certainly worthy of an entry in the database," he said. "That suit is absolutely amazing!"

"I wonder if we could make some suits like this for us?" Max asked. "Would we be able to get the design?"

"Of course," said Marc. "If I can help more people that would be wonderful."

They walked back toward Tower Bridge as they talked. Pausing for a moment outside the Tower of London, they saw the thieves being put into police cars, their hands cuffed together.

Li looked at her watch.

"We had better hurry," she told the others. It's going to be pretty busy getting through all the traffic around the Tower of London now."

"We really need to look at inventing something that could just transport us somewhere," said Max.

"Funny you should mention that," said Marc. "I've been thinking of a similar idea for a while and my next invention should be finished in a few months."

"Oh no," groaned Li. "Just make sure you contact us about it first next time!"

RIPLEY'S DATABASE ENTRY

RIPLEY FILE NUMBER : 54763

MISSION BRIEF : Believe it or not, a strange creature has been seen in the skies above London. Investigate accuracy of these accounts for Ripley database.

CODE NAME : The Birdman

REAL NAME : Marc Powell

LOCATION : London, England

AGE : 39

HEIGHT : 5 ft 10 in

WEIGHT : 154 lb

VIDEO CAPTURE

UNUSUAL CHARACTERISTICS :

Wears a suit that has huge, collapsible, fiberglass wings with mini gas-turbine engines strapped to them. When in flight, flames can be seen coming from the engines.

RBI DATABASE APPROVED!

INVESTIGATING AGENTS :

Max Johnson, Jack Stevens, Li Yong

▶▶ YOUR NEXT ASSIGNMENT

JOIN THE RBI IN THEIR NEXT ADVENTURE!

Sub-Zero Survival

Prologue

A cold wind blew fiercely across the frosty wilderness, where white mounds of snow covered everything in sight. Stars shone brightly in the black sky. With no human civilization for miles, there was no man-made light to pollute the brilliance of this night scene. A chilling gale moving in from the water whipped up the surface of this truly hostile land. A group of seals sensed the change in the wind and barked to each other, giving and receiving orders. Although this place was far too harsh for man, the seals thrived in the bitter, glacial conditions. One by one, the creatures moved toward the edge of the ice floe they were on and dropped into the biting cold water below.

A dark shape cut silently through the water headed for the seals: a killer whale, hungry for a meal. It targeted a small cluster of seals on

the edge of the group as its best option and set off through the icy sea toward them.

At the last moment, the whale changed its course. Some other creature had blocked its path, a pale body rising between the whale and its prey. The seals, sensing danger, began to bark again and scurried away. The confused whale backed off for now, realizing that this disruption had taken away the advantage of surprise and allowed its meal to escape.

As the whale disappeared back into the icy waters, the pale creature joined the group of seals again. The seals swam happily beside this newcomer, a creature quite uncommon in this land of ice, and unbelievable in the glacial water.

ENTER THE STRANGE WORLD OF RIPLEY'S ...

▶▶ Believe it or not, there is a lot of truth in this remarkable tale. The Ripley's team travels the globe to track down true stories that will amaze you. Read on to find out about real Ripley's case files and discover incredible facts about some of the extraordinary people and places in our world.

Ripley's
Believe It or Not!®

▶▶ JET MAN

credit: Anja Niedringhaus/AP/Press Association Images

An ex-airline pilot, Yves Rossy, doesn't need a plane to fly anymore. The daredevil from Switzerland can soar thousands of feet up in the air attached to his homemade wings powered by four miniature jet engines.

▶▶ The wings unfold automatically while he is airborne after jumping from a regular aircraft, before the jet turbines activate. He steers with his body weight and lands using a parachute.

▶▶ After leaping from a plane at 10,000 feet, Yves flew 22 miles across the English Channel in 2008, reaching speeds of over 186 miles an hour.

▶▶ Yves attempted to be the first person to fly between two continents—Africa and Europe, from Spain to Morocco—but hit turbulence and was forced to ditch into the sea in 2009.

TOWER BRIDGE

▶▶ Tower Bridge was built in 1894 when the population of the east side of the city increased so that another bridge, apart from London Bridge, was needed for people to cross the River Thames. It took eight years and 432 workers to build. The lower road is made up of two halves that can be raised to allow tall ships through.

BIG BEN

▶▶ Big Ben is a large clock that stands at the end of the Palace of Westminster. Built in 1859, the tower is over 315 feet high.

THE TOWER OF LONDON

▶▶ The Tower of London was built over 900 years ago by William the Conqueror. It stands 90 feet high and some walls are 11 feet thick. It was the tallest building in London for 212 years.

THE LONDON EYE

▶▶ The London Eye carries 800 passengers at a time, and from the top of the ride on a clear day you can see as far as 25 miles away. Each of the capsules weighs 10 tons and each rotation takes about 30 minutes. The wheel moves continuously, allowing passengers to step on and off without stopping.

CASE FILE #002

▶▶ CRYSTAL MINI

Artists Ken and Annie Burkitt from Canada covered every inch of a Mini Cooper car with one million Swarovski crystals that depict 11 American icons, such as the Statue of Liberty, the White House, and Mount Rushmore.

▶▶ It took a team of four people six months to attach the colorful crystals one by one.

▶▶ Despite the many sparkling additions, the car is still a fully functioning Mini Cooper.

▶▶ The artists have also covered a double-decker London bus in 100,000 gold-plated British pennies.

▶ FLIERS

PTEROSAURS

credit: Michael Burke/Rex Features

▶▶ Pterosaurs lived over 200 million years ago, and were some of the first animals to be able to fly. They included the largest creatures ever to get off the ground. *Hatzegopteryx* had an estimated wingspan of 40 feet and a head that measured 8 feet.

▶▶ The Arctic tern flies over 45,000 miles each year between the Arctic and the Antarctic, the longest migration of any bird. Over the possible 30-year lifetime of the bird, it can travel more than a million miles.

▶▶ The peregrine falcon is the fastest animal on earth. When seeking prey, it reaches speeds of more than 200 miles an hour during its "power-dive" (called a stoop), as it swoops down to catch its prey in mid-air.

▶▶ The great albatross, which ranges across the Southern Oceans, has the largest wingspan of any living bird, measuring up to 11 feet. It spends most of its life in the air and can glide for hours without beating its wings.

▶▶ The bar-tailed godwit, a Pacific coastal bird, makes flights of more than 6,800 miles without stopping to eat.

123

▶▶ WINGSUIT MAN

credit: Sipa Press/Rex Features

▶▶ The suit works on the same principles that allow small mammals such as flying foxes to soar through the air from tree to tree.

Skydiver Ueli Gegenschatz used a hi-tech suit with extra fabric between the arms and legs, which acted like the wings of a bird. He travelled for great distances with no propulsion other than the wind.

▶▶ Using only his wingsuit, Ueli flew an incredible 10.8 miles over the Irish Sea from Inis Mor island to the Irish mainland.

▶▶ It took Ueli only 5 minutes 45 seconds to reach Ireland at an average speed of 150 miles an hour—fast enough to beat a passenger plane flying the same route.

▶▶ Ueli jumped from a plane at 15,000 feet to complete his flight.

▶▶ In his lifetime, Ripley traveled over 450,000 miles looking for oddities—the distance from Earth to the Moon and back again.

▶▶ Ripley had a large collection of cars, but he couldn't drive. He also bought a Chinese sailing boat, called Mon Lei, but he couldn't swim.

▶▶ Ripley was so popular that his weekly mailbag often exceeded 170,000 letters, all full of weird and wacky suggestions for his cartoon strip.

▶▶ He kept a boa constrictor 20 feet long as a pet in his New York home.

▶▶ Ripley's Believe It or Not! cartoon is the longest-running cartoon strip in the world, read in 42 countries and 17 languages every day.

In 1918, Robert Ripley became fascinated by strange facts while he was working as a cartoonist at the *New York Globe*. He was passionate about travel and, by 1940, had visited no less than 201 countries, gathering artifacts and searching for stories that would be right for his column, which he named Believe It or Not!

Ripley bought an island estate at Mamaroneck, New York, and filled the huge house there with unusual objects and odd creatures that he'd collected on his explorations.

Check out the next amazing, action-packed adventure with the RBI team in ...

▶▶ Sub-Zero Survival